P9-DTN-674

Ken Griffey Jr.
&
Ken Griffey Sr.

by

Skip Press

CRESTWOOD HOUSE
Parsippany, New Jersey

Library of Congress Cataloging-in-Publication Data
Press, Skip
   Ken Griffey Jr. & Ken Griffey Sr. / by Skip Press.
     p.   cm. — (Star families)
   Includes index.
   ISBN 0-89686-881-8 (lsb.). —ISBN 0-382-39189-6 (pbk.)
     1. Griffey, Ken—Juvenile literature. 2. Griffey, Ken, 1950– —Juvenile literature. 3. Baseball players—United States—
Biography—Juvenile literature. [1. Griffey, Ken. 2. Griffey, Ken, 1950– . 3. Baseball players. 4. Afro-Americans—
Biography.] I. Title. II. Series: Press, Skip, 1950–   Star families.
GV865.A1P74 1996
796.357′092′2—dc20
[B]   95-11815

Summary: A joint biography of father and son baseball players Ken Griffey Jr. and Ken Griffey Sr.

Photo Credits
Cover: Focus on Sports
Allsport USA: 8
AP/Wide World: 4, 6, 13, 14, 17, 18, 21, 31, 34, 37, 38
Duomo: 28
Focus on Sports: 11, 19, 25, 29, 30, 33, 39, 41
Reuters/Bettmann: 21, 23, 27

Acknowledgments

The author would like to thank the following people for their contributions in compiling this book:
The Baseball Encyclopedia; Charles Whitaker and *Ebony* magazine; *Jet* magazine; Jack Friedman and *People* magazine;
Dan Dieffenback and *Sport* magazine; Hank Hersch, E.M. Swift, and *Sports Illustrated* magazine; and *U.S. News &
World Report*.

 Published by Crestwood House, a division of Simon & Schuster,
299 Jefferson Road, Parsippany, NJ 07054

Produced by Red Star Creative Services/Willmar, MN

Printed in the United States of America

First edition

10 9 8 7 6 5 4 3 2 1

Contents

Ken Griffey Jr. (left) jokes with his father, Ken Griffey Sr., on the Seattle Mariners' bench during a game with the Detroit Tigers.

Making History

On August 31, 1990, at the Seattle Kingdome, over 27,000 baseball fans witnessed a special occasion. Playing center field for the Seattle Mariners was their young star, Ken Griffey Jr. Next to him, in left field, was a special man that "Junior" had known all his life, a man who was now helping him make history.

Junior was only 20 years old and on his way to a tremendous season. He would finish the year with a .300 **batting average**, 22 **home runs**, 80 **runs batted in (RBIs)**, and 16 **stolen bases**. Junior was so popular that the "Ken Griffey Jr. Chocolate Bar" went on the market in the Pacific Northwest only three months after he joined the team, in the summer of 1989, and 800,000 candy bars were sold that year!

Only two other professional baseball players have had candy bars named after them: George Herman "Babe" Ruth was honored by the "Baby Ruth" candy bar, and Reggie "Mr. October" Jackson saw his name sweetly displayed on the "Reggie" bar. Both Ruth and Jackson had become famous while playing for the New York Yankees. Like them, Junior is an amazing home-run hitter who could surpass both Ruth and Jackson in career home runs. Unlike them, however, Junior can't eat the candy bar named after him. He is allergic to chocolate!

That summer night in 1990, though, nobody was thinking about chocolate bars. Home runs, maybe, but there was something even more important taking place. Joining Junior in the Seattle outfield on August 31, 1990, was a player with his own .300 lifetime batting average. The Mariners' new player had come out of retirement to play for the Seattle club, and the fans were going

5

wild. This new left fielder, you see, was Junior's *father*—Ken Griffey Senior—a man some thought would be elected to the **Baseball Hall of Fame**. Ken Senior was already the proud owner of two **World Series** championship rings, won during his years playing with the Cincinnati Reds. He was 40 years old, twice his son's age, as he trotted out to play alongside Junior.

Both Griffeys were grinning. In Junior's rookie year of 1989, they had become the first father/son combination ever to play in the major leagues at the same time—Ken Senior with the Cincinnati Reds and Junior with the Seattle Mariners. Now they had also become the first father-son pair ever to play *together* on the same team.

The Griffeys react during a television interview prior to their historic game together in 1990.

The Mariners club thought so highly of their budding **superstar** that the club management asked Junior's permission before signing Ken Senior. They didn't want to make Junior feel uncomfortable, even though Ken Senior was still a valuable player who would have been a fine addition to any club. Junior told the Mariner management that he was thrilled about the idea of playing with his dad. He also knew that having the two Griffeys playing together in the same outfield would be a big attraction for fans. With both Griffeys on the covers of team publications and national magazines, and appearing on talk shows to discuss their history-making outfield, that meant lots of ticket sales. And that was a nice thing to remind a team of when it came time to sign a new contract.

But no major-league team would draft any player, young or old, just to get fans into the ballpark. Ken Senior had to be able to play, and play well. Could he do the job? The manager of the Mariners, Jim Lefebvre, summed it up best.

"The reports we got said [Ken Senior] could still play," Lefebvre told *U.S. News & World Report*, "which is more important than having a father and son on the field to draw fans."

Of course, Lefebvre couldn't help but smile when the fans cheered over seeing Ken Senior as he stepped up to bat, with Junior waiting in the **on-deck circle**.

In times past, Junior would often **choke** at the plate when he knew his dad was watching. Normally a great hitter, Junior often failed to get a hit with his father looking on. That's embarrassing enough if you're a kid, but a hundred times worse if you are a major-league player!

This night was different, however. There was a charge in the air, an electric feeling that everyone in the stadium felt. Even the Kansas City Royals, the visiting team, knew this was a very special night.

Neither Griffey managed more than one hit on August 31, 1990, but one each was enough, because the hits came back to back: Ken Senior banged a **single**; then Junior did the same. Back-to-back hits for pro baseball's first father-and-son combination!

Even better, the Mariners went on to win the game, defeating the Royals, 5–2.

In March of 1994, the now-retired Ken Senior told Dan Dieffenback of *Sport* magazine that nothing in his career topped playing alongside Junior.

"I played baseball for nearly 20 years," Ken Senior said, "and playing with him was the number-one memory of my career. The time I played with him was special; it was emotional for me. On the field I was his teammate, off the field I was his father, and on the bench I was his coach."

It is understandable just how special those times were for Ken Griffey Senior. He had not been as lucky as Junior in the father department. In fact, Ken Senior's father had a lot to do with why Ken Senior worked so hard to see that Junior got a great start in life. Ken Griffey Senior, you see, barely knew his own father.

Ken Junior was thrilled to be able to play on the same major-league team as his father.

Making It in "The Show"

Named George Kenneth Griffey at his birth on April 10, 1950, young Ken was only two years old when his father, Buddy, abandoned the family. Left to make their own way in the world were Ken; his mother, Ruth; and five other children. It was not the most promising beginning in the little town of Donora, Pennsylvania. Yet Ruth somehow managed, supporting her children on welfare checks and whatever odd jobs she could find.

Seven years after he had left the family, Buddy showed up at their door. Not recognizing his father, young Ken closed the door in Buddy's face.

One of the greatest baseball players of all time—Stanley Frank "Stan The Man" Musial—had also been born in Donora and was a source of inspiration to the townspeople. In fact, Buddy Griffey had even played baseball with Musial in Donora, long before Stan the Man went on to star with the St. Louis Cardinals as one of the game's all-time best hitters. Though Buddy Griffey was not an inspiration to young Ken, Musial probably was. In any event, sports offered Ken Griffey a way out of poverty. A high school football and track star, Ken was also a fine baseball player—good enough, in fact, to be drafted in 1969 by the Cincinnati Reds.

The timing couldn't have been better, for the promising athlete became a father while still a teenager, at age 19. On November 21, 1969, Ken's wife, Alberta, gave birth to George Kenneth Griffey Jr., in Donora. Two years later, in 1971, son Craig was born. Ken vowed to "Bertie" (Alberta) that he would succeed where Buddy had failed. He would provide for his family and be a good dad, too.

Ken Griffey Sr. was drafted by the Cincinnati Reds in 1969.

It wasn't easy supporting a wife and a family as a baseball player. Ken Senior did not make a huge salary in the **minor leagues**, where he spent his first four and a half years in professional baseball. It was hard work, year-round. In the winter, he sharpened his skills in the **Puerto Rico League**. The time in the minors didn't bother Ken Senior, though, because he had more time to spend with his children.

"The days in the minor leagues were the best times because that's when I developed a closeness with them," Ken Senior told *Ebony* magazine in 1989. "I was always with them. I had them all the time."

Spending so much time with their father gave the boys an opportunity to learn about baseball. Junior learned too much at times, it seemed to Ken. Sitting in the dugout once, Junior overheard Ken Senior say about the pitcher for the other team, "[He's] got nothin'." The next time Ken Senior went up to bat, the pitcher with "nothin'" struck him out. When Ken Senior came back to the dugout, Junior exclaimed, "Dad, you got nothin'!" His father's teammates couldn't stop laughing.

In 1973, Ken was called up from the minor leagues to **The Show**, or the major leagues, for the first time, playing 25 games with the Cincinnati Reds. The next year he was with the Reds for 88 games, more than half the regular season. In 1975, he became a full-time player and immediately made an impression on the older stars on the club.

"[Ken Senior] was the best fastball hitter I had seen," Reds star and member of the Hall of Fame Joe Morgan recalled in *A Life in Baseball*. "It did not matter where you pitched him, in, out, up, or down, he was always able to handle heat [fast pitches]. He had speed, he could throw, he was smart in the outfield . . ."

Ken Senior scores on a home run in the third inning of a game against the Philadelphia Phillies in 1976.

Morgan called Ken Senior's addition to the club " a tremendous boost." It must have been, for in 1975 the club was so good they were known as "The Big Red Machine." They won their division, the National League West, an amazing 20 games ahead of their closest challenger. Morgan, Pete Rose, George Foster, and Ken Griffey Senior all hit .300 or better. Other great Reds players were Johnny Bench, Tony Perez, and Dave Concepcion. The team won six Western Division titles in a decade, five under the leadership of George "Sparky" Anderson and the sixth under John McNamara, and more total games and league titles than any other major league ball club. In an eight-year span, Reds players were selected as the National League's Most Valuable Player six times. An amazing 21 million fans came to Riverfront Stadium to see the Reds play in the 1970s. Today, The Big Red Machine is widely regarded as the greatest baseball team of its era.

As Joe Morgan remarked, Ken Senior was a large part of the Reds' success. During Ken's first nine years with the team, his batting average was .307, and his fielding was among the best in baseball. Griffey's and the Reds' greatest years came in 1975 and 1976, however. That's when they won the World Series two years in a row.

Ken Senior hits a triple in Game Six of the 1975 World Series.

Life on Top of the World

In 1975, the Cincinnati Reds were the only ball club in the Major Leagues to score more than 800 runs. If their offense wasn't enough, they also led in fielding! When they beat the Pittsburgh Pirates in the National League Championship Series, only the third game was close. But the World Series matchup against the Boston Red Sox was worthy of its title, the Fall Classic. Ken Senior batted a respectable .269 for the seven games, helping his team beat Carl Yastrzemski and the Boston Red Sox in what many sports fans believe was the best-played World Series in history. Ken Senior and the Reds were the heroes of Cincinnati as the city celebrated its first world championship in 35 years!

The next year the team won its division by "only" ten games. The 1976 National League Championship Series was not as easy for the Reds. Every one of their three straight victories against the Philadelphia Phillies was a nail-biter. In Game Two, on October 10, Ken Senior and Pete Rose had two hits each to lead their team to victory. In Game Three, Ken Senior hit a dramatic bouncing chopper off the glove of Phillies first baseman Bobby Tolan and started a three-run ninth-inning rally that put the Reds over the top. Griffey's .385 batting average for the series was topped only by Pete Rose's .429.

Ken Senior batted far worse in the World Series, which pitted the Reds against the New York Yankees, the **American League** champs. Through four games, Griffey managed only a dismal .059 average, but he scored the winning run in Game Two. Pete Rose, the team's superstar, didn't do much better, batting only .188. It didn't matter. Catcher Johnny Bench pounded out a startling .533 average, while George Foster hit .429 and five other Reds starters batted over .300.

15

It was the first time in 54 years that a National League team had won back-to-back World Series titles. The Reds became the first team since the leagues were broken into divisions to **sweep** both a League Championship and a World Series. The Reds so dominated the World Series that the Yankees held the lead in a game only once.

Despite his lackluster batting in the World Series, Ken Senior had a great year in 1976. He nearly won the **National League** batting title, only to be edged out by Bill Madlock of the Chicago Cubs, who finished with a .339 average on the final day of the season.

Unfortunately, things went downhill for the Red Machine after their second World Series title. The team won another division title in 1979 but lost in the National League Championship Series that year to the Pittsburgh Pirates.

Ken Senior's next big career success did not come until 1980. Playing in the **All-Star Game,** he hit a home run and was named **Most Valuable Player (MVP)** for the game! He was still riding high in 1981. With the best record in the National League, the Reds and Griffey appeared to be on their way back.

Then a baseball strike shortened the season.

Upset with the way some things were going in Cincinnati, Ken Senior got himself traded to the New York Yankees. It was a chance for him to have a "second career" and make even more of a name for himself. But there was one very big drawback. Playing in New York meant he would be away from his sons. He could no longer be "always with them" as he had been in the minors and at home in Cincinnati. The kids were settled in school and

Ken Senior accepts the Most Valuable Player award from Baseball Commissioner Bowie Kuhn at the end of the All-Star game in 1980.

Ken Senior got himself traded to the Yankees when he became upset with the way things were going in Cincinnati.

playing on their own sports teams. To move them to New York might be too upsetting. The Griffeys decided the boys and their mother would continue living in Ohio. Ken Senior would stay in New York during baseball season, with his family visiting him whenever possible. It was a tough period of adjustment, leaving Ken Senior wondering just how good a father he could be from a distance.

Ken Senior and his wife, Alberta, enjoy some free time between games.

Family Matters

Ken Senior had often taken his kids along to the ballpark in Cincinnati. Junior and Craig were friendly with the sons of other ball players and played in father-son games. That all changed when Ken was traded to New York. Ken kept in touch with his boys over the telephone and heard about their sports activities but was only able to see Junior play once or twice a year. Alberta picked up her husband's slack, advising Junior on his hitting and on baseball strategy.

Ken Senior's five seasons with the Yankees did not match his success with the Reds. He was sometimes used at first base and other times in the outfield, and injuries hampered his performance. Still, his batting average was only slightly less than it had been when he played with the Reds. What he had not counted on was the turmoil within the Yankees organization, which often affected its players.

In 1983, Junior and Craig were flown to New York to see their father play. With the Yankees way behind in the game and having little chance to win, some of the players' kids became bored and went to play dodgeball in the Yankees' clubhouse. The Yankees' manager, Billy Martin, was upset with Ken Griffey's play that day. So in a fit of anger, he ordered the Griffey kids—and only the Griffey kids—removed from the clubhouse. Ken Senior would not allow it. Later, at home in Ohio, Ken explained the incident and the troubles of the Yankees organization to his boys. He then advised them to try to forget about it.

If the other family members forgot about it, Junior didn't. As a 12-year-old Little Leaguer, he had been thrilled to have his father

Ken Senior was a great role model for Ken Junior, both as a father and a baseball player.

throw batting practice to him in Yankee Stadium. After the troubling incident with Billy Martin, Junior would not go back. He did not return to Yankee Stadium until he faced the Yankees as a professional in a baseball game.

Ken Senior managed to keep Junior and Craig in line, even if he had to spend $600 a month in long-distance phone calls to do it. Occasionally, when he felt it was needed, Ken Senior would fly his boys out to see him.

"If I needed to talk to him [Ken Senior], I would call him after the game," Junior told *Ebony* magazine. "If I did something wrong, he'd fly me to New York and say, 'You can't do that!' Then he would send me home the next day, and I'd play baseball."

Ken Senior didn't have to do much in the way of advising Junior on baseball, however. He told *Sport* magazine he had not bothered with Junior's baseball swing since Junior was nine years old. Junior was a natural talent. He was so talented, in fact, that by the time Junior was 16, Alberta told Ken on the phone that she thought Junior could hold his own in the **Connie Mack League,** playing with 18-year-olds. After all, the boy was excelling at both football and baseball for Moeller High School in Cincinnati. Junior was a multi-sport star just like his father. And when it came to baseball, Junior had something Ken Senior didn't—*power.* Enough hitting power that major-league scouts had even dropped by Junior's Little League games to watch.

Alberta's assessment of Junior's abilities was right. At age 16, Junior went off to play for the Midland Cardinals in the Connie Mack League. He led the Cardinals to the Connie Mack World Series and broke a number of league records. He kept in touch with his parents every night by making collect long-distance phone calls from the coach's room.

Junior's talents continued to grow. He was usually the best player on the field—unless his dad was watching from the stands. For some reason, Junior seemed to choke when Ken Senior

In 1987 Ken Junior was the Major League Baseball number one draft pick.

watched him play. It got so bad that before one big game for Moeller High, Junior's coach called Ken Senior and asked him not to come to the game. The coach reasoned that there would be dozens of scouts for colleges and professional teams at the game to watch Junior, and the coach didn't want his star player jinxed!

In 1987, the Griffey family had a very proud day. Junior was the number-one player—out of a field of 1,263—in the Major League Baseball **draft** by the Seattle Mariners. He received a **signing bonus** of $160,000—not bad for a kid who had just graduated from high school!

At the time, the Mariners were the worst team in baseball. Neither Junior nor his father liked the idea of Junior playing there, but that was the luck of the draft. So, with his $160,000 check in his back pocket, Junior said goodbye to his family at the Cincinnati airport and headed off to his first stop on the way to The Show. His first assignment was the Class A farm club (minor-league team) of the Mariners, located in Bellingham, Washington.

Ken Junior started out in a minor league team of the Seattle Mariners.

Young Man in a Hurry

Usually, a baseball player trying to make it in the major leagues starts out on a minor-league team, proves his ability and learns, and is then promoted to the majors.

When Junior joined the Bellingham Mariners, he was a kid in a hurry. Seventeen-year-old Junior wanted to make it to The Show by age 18. Maybe he was in too much of a hurry. His batting average fell to .230. He became depressed and stayed out too late, trying to lift his spirits. So he was benched for breaking curfew. He called his mother and told her that he felt like quitting. It didn't matter that he had a brand-new BMW or lots of money in the bank.

Alberta reminded Junior that it had taken Ken Senior four and a half years to make it to the majors. She also advised Junior to stop trying to hit a home run every time he came to bat and to just try and get a hit instead. She also reminded him how much money the Mariners had already invested in him.

The pressure on Junior got to be too much. "It seemed like everyone was yelling at me in baseball," he told a reporter for *Jet* magazine in April of 1992. "Then I came home and everyone was yelling at me there. I got depressed. I got angry. I didn't want to live." Ken Griffey Jr. became so depressed that he attempted suicide by swallowing 277 aspirin tablets. He was rushed to Providence Hospital in Mount Airy, Ohio, where he recovered in the intensive care unit. For a long time, he would not talk about that dark period in his life, but now he counsels other youngsters who may be contemplating this "wrong way out."

After recovering from that low point, Junior hit .450 for the rest of the season, finishing the year with a .320 average, 14 home runs, and 13 stolen bases. He was immediately promoted to the Class A San Bernardino Spirit team, in California.

Ken Junior overcame some rough times early in his career to become one of the most talented players in the game.

Ken Senior at the plate for the Atlanta Braves.

By this time, Ken Senior was playing with the Atlanta Braves. After a game against the Dodgers in Los Angeles, Ken drove out to San Bernardino to see his son play. He brought some new bats along as a present. This time, Junior didn't choke. After all, he was leading the California League in hitting, with a .520 average. The announcer opened the game by asking the crowd—"What time is it?" "It's Griffey time!" they yelled. Junior did quite well at the plate that night, even hitting a home run. The event was chronicled in an article in *Sports Illustrated* magazine.

The jinx was broken, and Ken Senior was impressed. He told his wife on the phone, "It doesn't make sense for someone to have that much talent!"

In half a season with the Spirit, Junior averaged .338, with 11 home runs and 42 RBIs. He was promoted to Seattle's Class AA Vermont team for the rest of the season. Unfortunately, he sprained his back. But he recovered in time to lead his team to the 1988 Eastern League playoffs, where he batted .444 and drove in seven runs.

Ken Junior overcame his jinx and turned into a powerful hitter.

There is one more level in professional minor-league baseball—Triple A. Junior was doing so well that he jumped past this level after finishing the season with Vermont. In February of 1989, he reported to spring training in The Show. He was now playing with the Seattle Mariners, wearing number 24—the number worn by his idol, Rickey Henderson. Junior set two major-league spring-training records: He collected 33 hits and 21 RBIs. Manager Jim Lefebvre quietly informed Junior that he was the Mariners' new starting center fielder: He had made it to the major leagues at the tender age of 20.

Ken Junior runs the baseline after hitting a home run.

Ken Junior jokes with his dad next to a poster of them in their team uniforms.

At the same time, Ken Senior was again playing for the Cincinnati Reds. Commenting to *People* magazine about his son's success, Griffey said, "I never had any idea this would happen—I never pushed him."

Junior agreed. "Dad never pushed me into anything," he told *Boys' Life* magazine. "He just told me to do whatever I wanted— football, basketball, baseball. He was just a dad."

Junior was so talented that Ken Senior didn't have to push. That talent showed early. As Ken Senior told *People*: "After age 12, I couldn't strike him out."

Neither could some major-league pitchers. In Junior's first **at-bat** in the Kingdome, he slammed a home run. In his first **pinch-hitting** appearance, in May of 1989, he hit a two-run homer to win the game. On June 4 in the Kingdome, facing his first knuckleball pitcher—Charlie Hough of the Texas Rangers— Junior smashed another homer.

Gene Clines, the Mariners' hitting coach, had high praise for the young star. "I don't think anybody's ever been that good at that age," Clines said. "He's in his own category. He is a natural."

Junior even got some revenge against the Yankees—he'd never forgotten their shabby treatment of him from years before. On April 26, the Cincinnati Reds were idle, so Ken Senior flew to New York to watch the Mariners take on the Yankees. The highlight of Junior's fine play was a spectacular catch that robbed Yankee Jesse Barfield of his 200th career home run. Though he didn't know it until that play, Ken Senior just happened to be sitting next to Barfield's wife in the stands.

Junior seemed a shoo-in for Rookie of the Year honors until he broke a bone in his left hand after slipping in the shower. He was disabled from July 24 to August 20. When he returned to the lineup, he tried too hard.

"I was worrying about hitting the ball 700 feet," he told E.M. Swift of *Sports Illustrated.* "I just wanted 20 home runs."

Once again, long-distance phone consultations with his mother and father helped Junior get his game back in shape. He finished third in the balloting for Rookie of the Year, finishing the season with a .264 average, 61 RBIs, and 16 stolen bases in 127 games played.

No one in the family was happy over the circumstances that had caused Junior to have a season he found personally disappointing, but they encouraged him to forget the past and look to the future. Little did Junior or anyone in the family know how amazing the next year would be, or how the Griffeys—Senior and Junior—would make the sports-history books in a way that might never be equaled.

The Griffeys pose for a 1989 promo shot in their respective team uniforms.

Ken Junior with his dad at a press conference announcing Ken Senior's new contract with the Mariners. It was the first time in major league baseball history that a father and son would be playing for the same team at the same time.

The Griffey Dynasty

In 1990, Ken Senior was released by the Cincinnati Reds at mid-season. It was a big disappointment for Griffey, but it set things in motion in Seattle. The Mariners had still not had a winning season. Team management was in the process of over-hauling the team's entire image. What if part of the Mariners' new look included the first father-son duo playing professional base-ball in the same outfield? Would it possibly work?

Would it ever!

When Ken Senior joined the Mariners, Junior was already used to being compared with his father. "It's harder being a son when your father is a baseball player," he told *Ebony* magazine in 1989. "People will say, 'Your dad hit .300 lifetime, so you have to hit .310 to be better.' They put you in a category with your father, and that's not fair because you are two different people."

As a team, however, the Griffeys were incomparable. Ask California Angels' pitcher Kirk McCaskill, who provided the Griffeys their most memorable moment in baseball.

It was two weeks after they had hit back-to-back singles in their first game together. On September 14, 1990—with a count of no balls and two strikes—Ken Senior pounded a 420-foot home run off McCaskill.

"That's how you do it, Son!" he exclaimed as he crossed the plate and slapped hands with Junior.

Junior stepped into the batter's box and waited. Finally, with the count at three balls and no strikes, he looked over at Jim Lefebvre and got the swing-away signal. He swung hard at the next pitch, banging a 388-foot homer into the record books—the first-ever father-and-son back-to-back home runs!

"I hit it solid and knew it was going out," Junior recalled later. "I looked over at Dad, and he couldn't believe it. I circled the bases, then trotted into the dugout and hugged him." Junior called it his most memorable experience at bat.

Junior finished the season hitting .300, with 22 homers, 80 RBIs, and 16 stolen bases. Ken Senior hit .377 for the Mariners, prompting them to sign him to a new one-year contract. For Junior, they did a little better, offering him a $2,000,000 two-year pact, which was much better than his $210,000 salary the year before!

The move by Seattle management paid off in more than ticket sales. The Mariners finished the 1991 campaign with a good showing, finishing with an 83–79 record, or a winning percentage of .512. It was the first winning season in the history of the franchise. Junior had a .327 average, 22 homers, 100 RBIs, and 18 stolen bases, while Ken Senior had a .282 average in only 85 at-bats.

The 1991 season was Ken Senior's last season and a respectable end to a long career. By the time Ken Senior retired, Junior was firmly established as a baseball superstar. And in 1991, the Mariners signed brother Craig to one of their minor-league teams. It seemed to be a dynasty-in-the-making.

Since his signing with the Mariners in 1987, Junior had grown taller and added muscle and strength. When Ken Senior retired, the question was not "How good is Junior?" but "Just how good can he be?"

The baseball world would soon find out.

Racing for the Record Books

At the age of 23 years, 6 months, and 25 days, Junior became the sixth youngest player in major-league baseball history to reach 100 career home runs. Four other players on that list are in the Hall of Fame: Hank Aaron, Eddie Mathews, Mel Ott, and Ken Senior's old Reds teammate Johnny Bench. Junior was selected for the All-Star team five straight years, from 1990 to 1994. At the 1992 All-Star Game in San Diego, he batted 1.000 and was named the game's "Most Valuable Player."

In 1993 Junior hit 109 RBIs—the third consecutive season he hit more than 100 RBIs—putting him in a unique club. He also tied the major-league record by hitting a home run in eight consecutive games. He finished the year with a .309 average in 582 at-bats, with 45 home runs and 17 stolen bases.

Ken Junior holds his trophy after winning the Most Valuable Player award at the 1992 All-Star Game in San Diego.

Ken Junior (left) shares a laugh with teammate Harold Reynolds (right) after the two were presented with Gold Glove awards in 1991.

In addition to numbers like that on offense, Junior has shown equally amazing talent on defense. A four-time **Gold Glove** winner for fielding excellence, he established in 1993 a new American League fielding record by making 573 **errorless chances** over 240 games. That means that every chance he had to catch a ball hit his way, he made the catch and he fielded all balls that were hit in his direction.

"I love to play defense because it's just you and the ball, a race," Junior told Dan Dieffenback of *Sport* magazine. "You could always go into a hitting slump, but I could never stop playing defense."

Junior truly deserves being called Seattle's **franchise player**, which is why the Mariners signed him to a lucrative contract through 1996. Hollywood moviemakers also took advantage of his popularity and cast him (as himself) in the movie *Little Big League.*

The year 1994 had the potential to be the greatest year ever for Ken Griffey Jr. It began with great joy, as Trey Kenneth Griffey was born to Junior and his wife, Melissa. The arrival of Junior's first child must have been inspiring, because Junior immediately embarked on an amazing year. On May 23, before the end of the first two months of the season, Junior pounded out his twenty-first home run, off the Oakland Athletics' Bobby Witt, breaking a record set by Mickey Mantle of the New York Yankees in 1956. (Coincidentally, that same day Junior passed Ken Senior's career home-run total of 152.) Many speculated that Junior might break Yankee Roger Maris's season home-run record of 61. A graph underneath Junior's picture on the cover of *Sports Illustrated* showed the possibility: By May, Junior had hit 29 homers, compared to Maris's 13 in the same time period. Ten days before the end of June, Junior hit number 30, off Brian Anderson of the California Angels, breaking a 66-year-old record for homers hit before June 30, set by Babe Ruth.

1994 was a banner year for Ken Junior.

By the time Junior appeared in the 1994 All-Star Game at Three Rivers Stadium in Pittsburgh, he had produced 33 home runs—an amazing feat. His batting average was .329. He received 6,079,688 fan votes to the All-Star team, 1.8 million more than any player had ever received! His manager in Seattle, ex-Yankee Lou Piniella, said, "I'd pay to see him play. He's the best in the game right now. All I have to do is put him in the lineup. . . . We were in Kansas City last week, and the fans gave him a standing ovation. I mean, that's when you've become a star."

Then disaster struck, but this time it wasn't a slump or an injury. Just as his father had faced a shortened baseball season due to a strike in 1981, Junior now had to deal with a major league labor dispute.

Rumors of a strike had loomed for months. Now it was looking all too real. The fans—including sportswriters, of course—prayed it wouldn't happen. *Sports Illustrated* put Junior and another power hitter, Frank Thomas, of the Chicago White Sox, on its August 8 cover. "Top Guns Frank Thomas and Ken Griffey Jr.," read the cover, "Two powerful reasons to keep playing ball." "Junior Comes of Age," said the headline on the article inside. As the magazine piece pointed out, "Ken Griffey Jr. has matured into more than a star—he's the new straw that stirs the game."

And so it went, but the strike was on. For the first time since the early part of the twentieth century, baseball closed out its season, with no World Series to offer the fans. By the time the season ended, in mid-August, several players were threatening Roger Maris's home-run record. In the National League, Matt Williams of the San Francisco Giants had 43 home runs, Jeff Bagwell of the Houston Astros had 39, and Barry Bonds of the San

40

Francisco Giants had 37. In the American League, Albert Belle of the Cleveland Indians had 36, Frank Thomas of the Chicago White Sox had 38, and Junior finished on top with 40. His fortieth homer was also his second **grand slam** of the season.

Making it tougher for Junior and his teammates was the fact that pieces of the roof of the Seattle Kingdome had literally began falling, forcing the team to play in other stadiums. Disgruntled, Junior told the *Wall Street Journal* that he expected the team to move to Tampa, Florida, by 1997. The strike and the dissatisfaction with conditions involving the team was a strange reminder of what had happened to Ken Senior back in Cincinnati.

The Griffeys both had similar experiences during their baseball careers.

Reflecting on the strike-shortened 1994 season, and his and Frank Thomas's lost chances to break records, Junior told *Sports Illustrated*, "We picked a bad year to have a good year." Still, it was a pretty good "bad" year. Junior finished with a .323 average (eighth in the American League) in 433 at-bats over 111 games—not bad numbers for anyone, especially for a player not even 25 years old.

When Ken Griffey Junior's career finally ends, he undoubtedly will have broken more records and maybe even have won a World Series or two, like his father. But now that Junior has his own son, there's little chance his values will change.

"Baseball isn't real life," he said early in 1994. "Family and friends, that's life. People don't understand that this game can drive you crazy if you let it, but it's not important compared to other things in life. My father taught me that, because he never brought it home. Whatever happened at the ballpark stayed at the ballpark."

If only it were true for everyone involved in the game of professional baseball. No matter how many records the Griffeys set on the field, one thing is certain: When it comes to families, they are definitely big league.

Glossary

All-Star Game A game played at the midpoint of the Major League Baseball season in which star players from the National League play against star players from the American League.

American League The younger of the two leagues of teams that comprise Major League Baseball.

at-bat In baseball, the opportunity for the batter to face the pitcher.

Baseball Hall of Fame A museum and shrine for the game of baseball and its greatest players located in Cooperstown, New York. The highest honor a professional baseball player or anyone involved with the game can receive is to become a member of the Hall of Fame.

batting average The percentage of hits a batter gets, calculated against the number of at-bats. For example, if a batter got four chances at bat during a game and got a hit in two of those at-bats, the batting average would be .500. Walks, granted when a pitcher throws four pitches out of the strike zone before throwing three in the strike zone, do not count in figuring one's batting average.

choke A slang term which implies that one is tensing up and suffering from diminished performance, particularly in times of high stress when the outcome of a game depends on the player's next action.

Connie Mack League A league for young baseball players aspiring to play professionally, named after Cornelius McGillicuddy "Connie" Mack, a famous baseball personality from the early part of the twentieth century.

draft   The selection of young athletes by professional sports teams who have won exclusive rights to choose these athletes.

errorless chance   An opportunity to field a baseball that is successfully completed. An example is a fly ball hit into the outfield that is caught by an outfielder, thus making an "out" of the opposing player who hit the ball. The American League recordholder for most successful errorless chances (573 over 240 games) is Ken Griffey Jr.

franchise player   A sports term for a player so outstanding that an entire franchise (professional team) can prosper and come to prominence with that athlete's talents. Good examples are Michael Jordan of the Chicago Bulls and Ken Griffey Jr. of the Seattle Mariners.

Gold Glove   The award given each year for the best fielders at their positions in the American and National leagues.

grand slam   A home run hit with the bases loaded.

home run   A hit beyond the reach of a fielder, within the boundary lines that signify the field of play, enabling the batter to circle all four bases in baseball and score a run without being challenged by a fielder.

minor leagues   Professional baseball teams where young players hone their skills to become major-league players. There are three levels of the minor leagues: A, AA, and AAA, with the latter being only one step away from the major leagues.

Most Valuable Player (MVP)   The player voted to be the one who made the greatest contribution to his team during the season or a game (such as the All-Star Game).

National League   The older of the two leagues that comprise Major League Baseball.

on-deck circle The place where the player waiting to come to bat stands.

pinch-hitting Batting in place of the regularly scheduled batter, especially when a hit is badly needed.

Puerto Rico League A league for Puerto Ricans and for professional baseball players from other countries. Games in this league are played during the winter, which is the "off-season" for professional baseball.

runs batted in (RBIs) Runs that are scored as the direct result of hits or sacrifices.

The Show The slang term that minor-league professional baseball players use for the Major Leagues, which consist of the National and American Leagues.

signing bonus Generally, a large sum of money given to an athlete as a bonus for signing his or her first professional contract. The size of the bonus is usually directly proportional to the estimated skills of the athlete and what he or she can contribute to the team.

single A hit with which a batter is able to advance to the first of three bases in baseball and no further. With a "double," the batter makes it to the second base, and to the third with a "triple."

stolen base A base achieved by a base runner not by a hit or walk but by running to the next base without getting tagged by a fielder holding the baseball.

superstar An athlete or performer who shows exceptional talent and public appeal far above that of his or her peers.

sweep To win a consecutive number of games in a given series with no losses.

World Series A series of games played by the winner of the National League Championship against the winner of the American League Championship. The first team to win four games in the series, which can go as many as seven games, becomes the World Series champion.

Index